NORTH AMERICAN DINOSAURS

STENONYCHOSAURUS

ANASTASIA SUEN

Rourke Educational Media
A Division of Carson Dellosa Education
rourkeeducationalmedia.com

ROURKE'S
SCHOOL to HOME
CONNECTIONS
BEFORE AND DURING READING ACTIVITIES

Before Reading: *Building Background Knowledge and Vocabulary*

Building background knowledge can help children process new information and build upon what they already know. Before reading a book, it is important to tap into what children already know about the topic. This will help them develop their vocabulary and increase their reading comprehension.

Questions and Activities to Build Background Knowledge:

1. Look at the front cover of the book and read the title. What do you think this book will be about?
2. What do you already know about this topic?
3. Take a book walk and skim the pages. Look at the table of contents, photographs, captions, and bold words. Did these text features give you any information or predictions about what you will read in this book?

Vocabulary: *Vocabulary Is Key to Reading Comprehension*

Use the following directions to prompt a conversation about each word.

- Read the vocabulary words.
- What comes to mind when you see each word?
- What do you think each word means?

Vocabulary Words:

- *asteroid*
- *asymmetrical*
- *balance*
- *descendants*
- *flesh*
- *fossil*
- *mammals*
- *reptile*
- *sacs*
- *wounding*

During Reading: *Reading for Meaning and Understanding*

To achieve deep comprehension of a book, children are encouraged to use close reading strategies. During reading, it is important to have children stop and make connections. These connections result in deeper analysis and understanding of a book.

Close Reading a Text

During reading, have children stop and talk about the following:

- Any confusing parts
- Any unknown words
- Text to text, text to self, text to world connections
- The main idea in each chapter or heading

Encourage children to use context clues to determine the meaning of any unknown words. These strategies will help children learn to analyze the text more thoroughly as they read.

When you are finished reading this book, turn to the next-to-last page for **Text-Dependent Questions** and an **Extension Activity**.

TABLE OF CONTENTS

THE STRANGE TOOTH

Dr. Ferdinand Hayden

In 1855, Dr. Ferdinand Hayden found a **fossil** of a strange-looking tooth in Montana. The tooth was smaller than a dime. But it had lots of sharp ridges. What could it be? He sent the tooth to Dr. Joseph Leidy.

When the strange tooth arrived in Philadelphia, Leidy thought it was a **reptile** tooth. He thought the tooth had belonged to a large lizard. In 1856, he named the creature *Troodon formosus*. *Troodon* means "**wounding** tooth." *Formosus* is Latin for "beautiful."

A Dinosaur!

As it turns out, the tooth wasn't from a lizard. It was one of the first dinosaur fossils found in the United States. What was the dinosaur's name? It's a long story! A clear answer would not come for over 150 years.

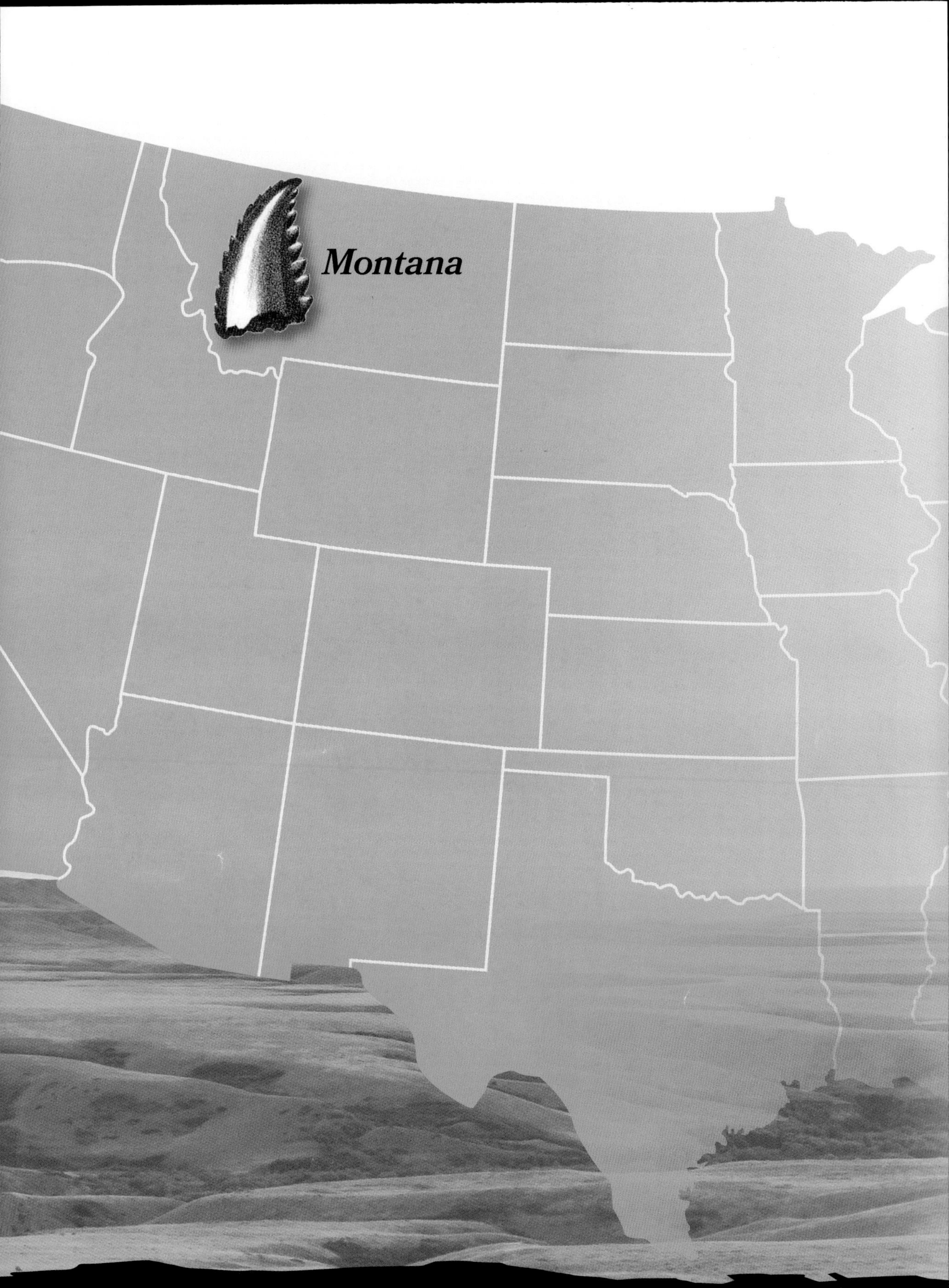
Montana

Men and women go out to dig up fossils every summer. They study plants and animals buried deep in the rocks. This is the science of paleontology.

How do they figure out what they dug up? Scientists look at the clues. They make notes about how far down they had to dig. They bring the bones back and study them.

For a long time, no one knew what this dinosaur looked like. It was hard to figure that out from just a tooth. But for years, that is what they found—more teeth.

MORE FOSSIL HUNTERS

Charles H. Sternberg was a famous fossil hunter. He started collecting fossils after he moved to Kansas as a teen. His three sons also hunted fossils with him. Levi, George, and Charles M. grew up in Kansas. All four men moved to Canada to dig up fossils.

This team of father and sons collected fossils for the Geological Survey of Canada. They took photographs of their work with glass plates. Charles M. signed his photos as C. M. Sternberg.

In 1932, C. M. found an unusual claw. The bones on the claw were different sizes. He named the creature *Stenonychosaurus inequalis*. *Stenonychosaurus* means "narrow claw lizard." *Inequalis* means "uneven."

Charles Mortram Sternberg

At long last, *Stenonychosaurus* (ste-NON-ik-oh-SAWR-us) had been found! But that was not the end of the story. In 1987, Dr. Philip Currie decided that these bones needed a different name. He changed the name to *Troodon formosus*. He changed it back to the name given when the first tooth was found in 1855.

Thirty years went by. Then in 2017, one of Currie's students found more bones. Aaron J. van der Reest compared the new bones with the old bones. They were not the same!

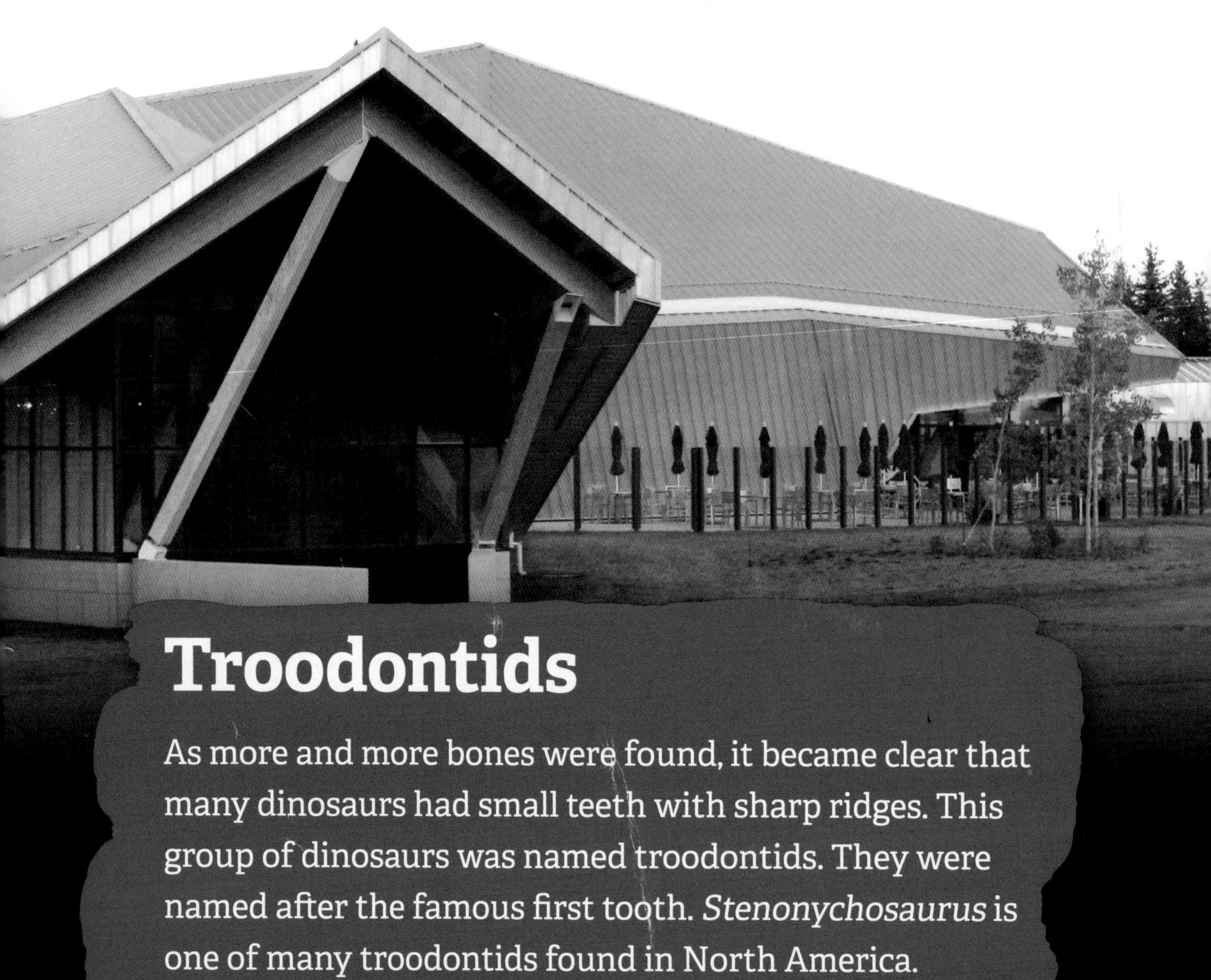

Troodontids

As more and more bones were found, it became clear that many dinosaurs had small teeth with sharp ridges. This group of dinosaurs was named troodontids. They were named after the famous first tooth. *Stenonychosaurus* is one of many troodontids found in North America.

Some of the new bones were like the old ones. Some of the new bones were different. He had found two different dinosaurs.

Van der Reest gave the two dinosaurs different names. He gave all of the matching bones the old name. He brought back the *Stenonychosaurus* name. The name was changed back. An old dinosaur name was now a new dinosaur name. The name *Troodon formosus* is no longer used.

Visitors to the Philip J. Currie Dinosaur Museum in Alberta, Canada, can take a tour of the Pipestone Creek bone bed nearby.

FROM HEAD TO TOE

As more fossils were found, the pieces of the puzzle began to come together. The skull held a very important clue.

Stenonychosaurus had a long skull. It had many small teeth in its long jaws. It also had the biggest head and brain for its size of any dinosaur. It was probably the smartest dinosaur. Why do scientists think so? Its brain was like an ostrich's brain.

OSTRICH

Most dinosaur brains are like reptile brains. An ostrich is smarter than any reptile. Was *Stenonychosaurus* an early version of a bird? Some scientists think so.

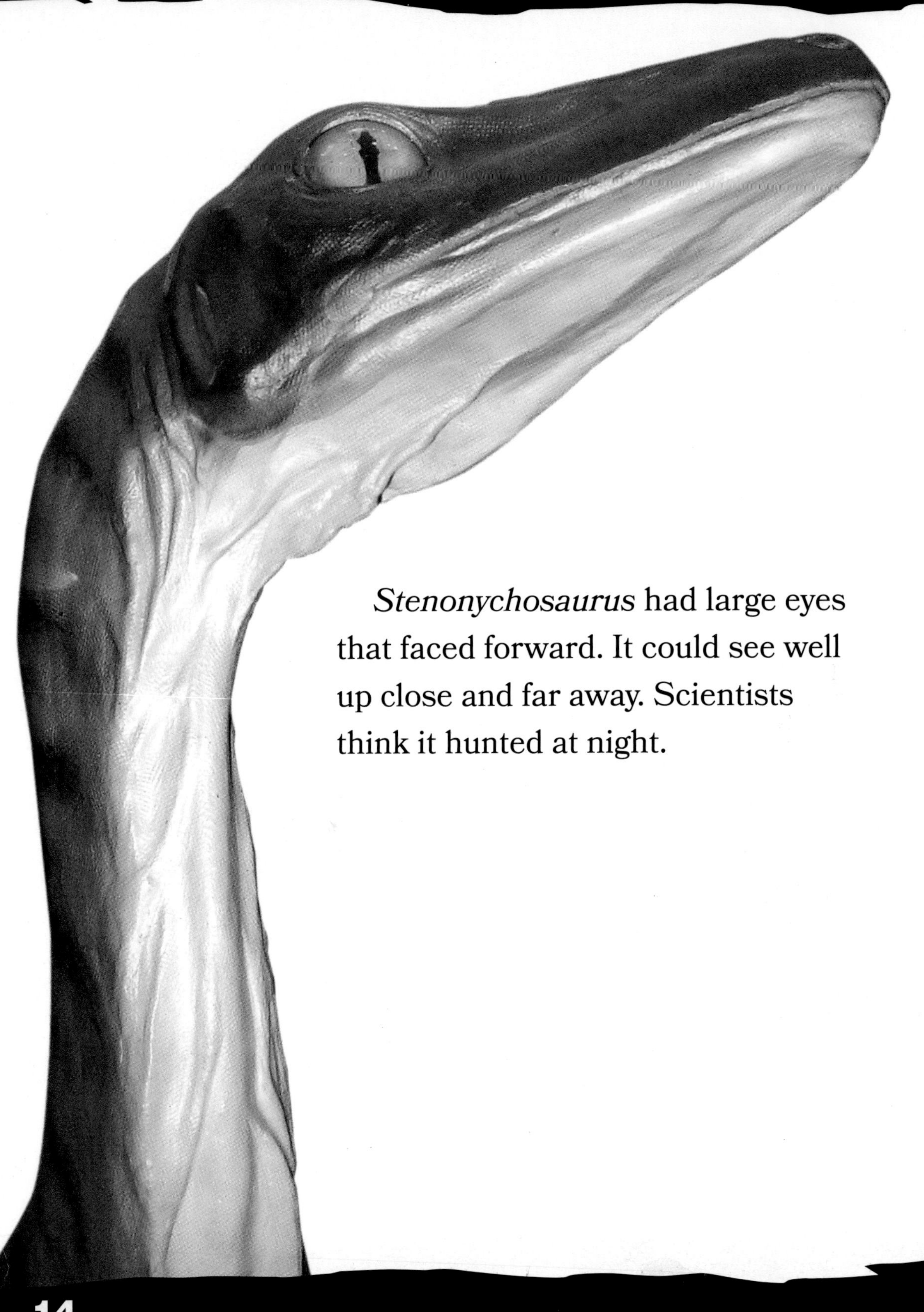

Stenonychosaurus had large eyes that faced forward. It could see well up close and far away. Scientists think it hunted at night.

The front part of this dinosaur's face was U-shaped. Its nose was fairly small. It probably used its sense of sight more than its sense of smell.

A grown *Stenonychosaurus* was about the size of a small adult human. It was about 6.5 feet (2 meters) long. It stood about 4.5 feet (1.4 meters) tall. It probably weighed about 100 pounds (45 kilograms).

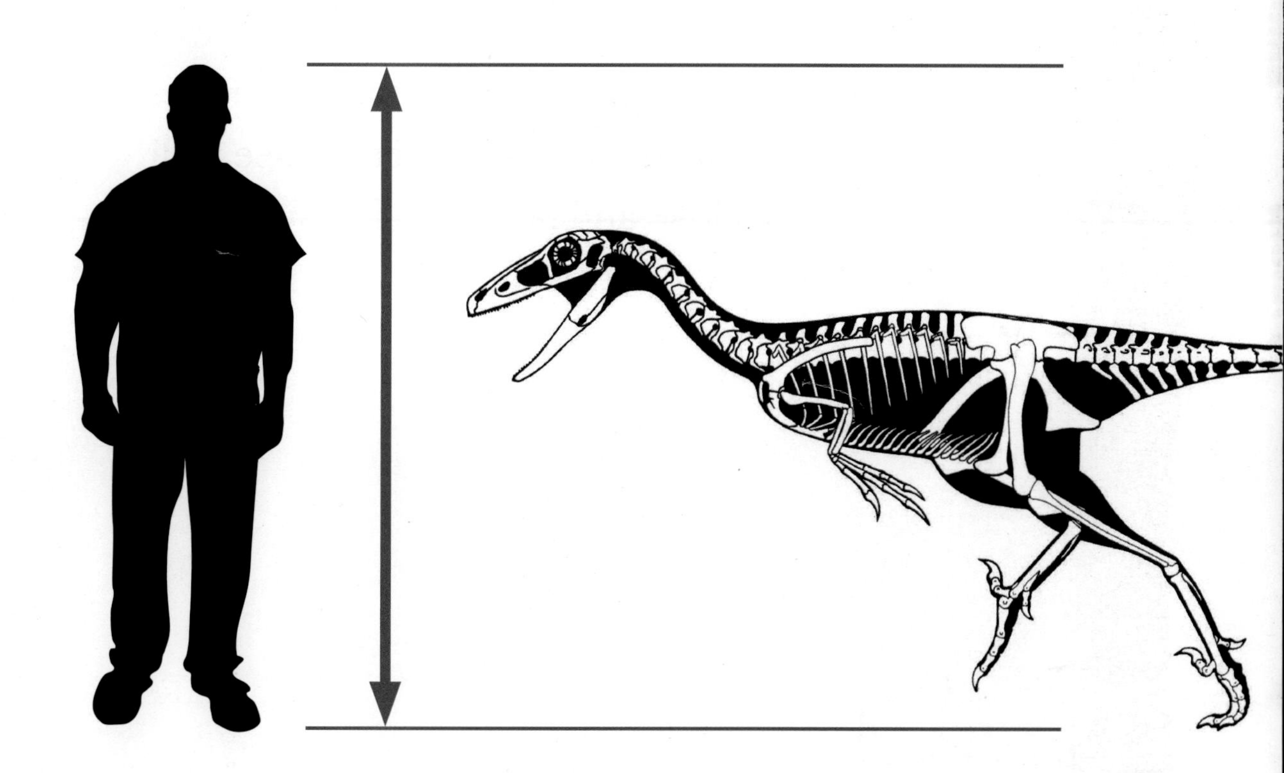

Stenonychosaurus had a long neck. Its arms and legs were long too. *Stenonychosaurus* also had a long, stiff tail.

Stenonychosaurus walked or ran on its two legs. It moved quickly to catch food. It used its big tail for **balance**. The tail also helped *Stenonychosaurus* turn quickly.

Experts aren't sure what the skin was like. It might have had feathers like a bird or scales like a lizard.

Feathers

In 2017 another new troodontid, *Jianianhualong tengi*, was found in China. This fossil had feathers on the arms, legs, back, and tail. The tail feathers were **asymmetrical**. One side of the feather was short, and the other side was long. Experts say that probably meant that this dinosaur could not fly.

TROODONTIDS

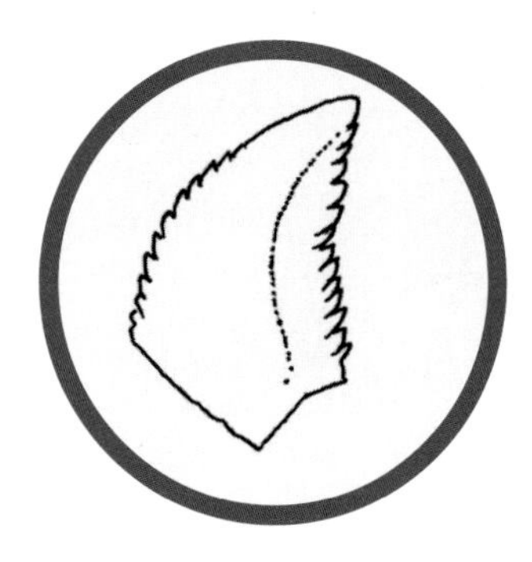

ZANABAZAR JUNIOR
Length: 10 feet (3 meters)

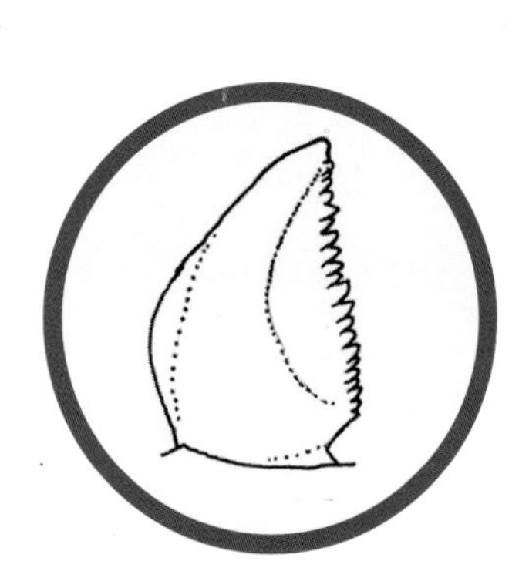

SINORNITHOIDES YOUNGI
Length: 3.5 feet (1.1 meters)

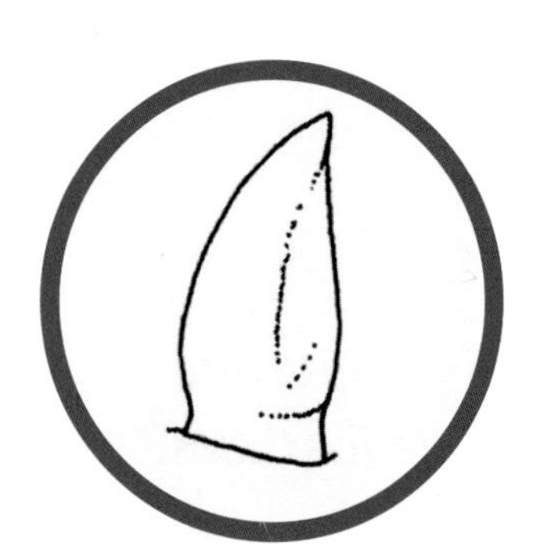

BYRONOSAURUS JAFFEI
Length: 4.9 feet (1.5 meters)

Stenonychosaurus had a claw on each hand that was like a thumb. It could use these claws to grab food.

The feet had three sharp claws that pointed forward. Another claw was on the side. This claw might have pulled back into the foot, like a cat claw. This probably helped this dinosaur run fast.

Stenonychosaurus could use this foot claw when it was needed. It may have helped the dinosaur protect itself. It may have helped it catch food.

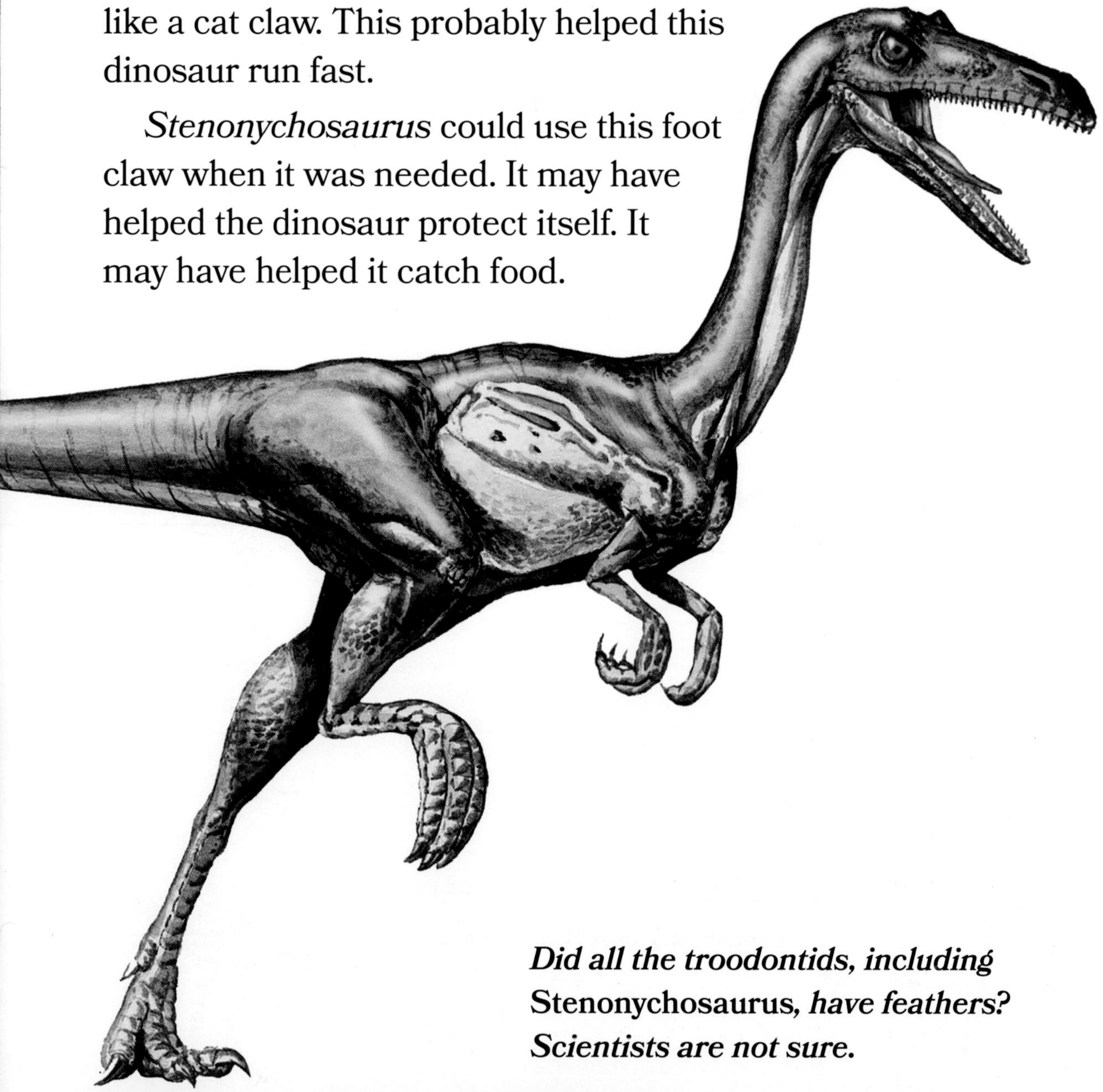

Did all the troodontids, including* Stenonychosaurus, *have feathers? Scientists are not sure.

DAILY LIFE

Stenonychosaurus had teeth with sharp edges that could tear **flesh**. They were the teeth of a meat eater. Most meat eaters can't be too choosy. *Stenonychosaurus* probably ate anything it could catch, such as lizards and snakes.

Stenonychosaurus also ate baby dinosaurs and dinosaur eggs. Its teeth have been found with baby hadrosaurs, which were duck-billed dinosaurs. It probably also ate early **mammals**.

Omnivores?

Scientists have also found troodontids with smooth back teeth. Did these dinosaurs also eat plants? Were they plant eaters and meat eaters? Were they omnivores? No one knows yet.

Some of today's plants were alive in prehistoric times. There were beech trees, fig trees, and roses. There were ferns and some grasses. There were gingko trees and cedar trees. There were oak, elm, and maple trees. There were redwood trees.

All those plants were food for plant eaters. More plant eaters meant that there was more food for meat eaters to enjoy!

Stenonychosaurus laid eggs, two at a time. Scientists have found 12 pairs of long eggs together. The mother laid the eggs in a dirt nest.

Scientists have also found parts of *Stenonychosaurus* lying on top of its eggs. This tells us that the parents guarded their eggs. They might have sat on the eggs to keep them warm.

The fossils of both old and young dinosaurs have been found together. *Stenonychosaurus* probably stayed in family groups after their young were born. The parents might have guarded their young. Maybe the family hunted together.

These dinosaur eggs became fossils.

Stenonychosaurus lived 75 million years ago. Many other dinosaurs were living during the same time. Now they are all gone.

Or are they? Scientists say that birds are living dinosaurs. Are the **descendants** of *Stenonychosaurus* still here? Did they turn into birds? No one is quite sure.

Stenonychosaurus and Birds

Birds might have come from dinosaurs such as *Stenonychosaurus*. Many things about birds and *Stenonychosaurus* are alike.

- Its middle ear was shaped like a bird's.
- Its teeth were smaller than older dinosaurs' teeth. Birds don't have teeth. Small teeth could have been a step toward having no teeth.
- Its brain had air **sacs**, and so do birds' brains.
- Its wrist moved sideways, just like birds and bats move their wings.

SECRETARY BIRD
TROODONTID

The Cretaceous Period ended 65 million years ago. *Stenonychosaurus* and many other animals died then. Why did that happen?

The latest scientific thinking is that dinosaurs and other animals died from more than one cause.

Here are some possibilities:

- An **asteroid** crashed into Mexico about 65 million years ago. It caused dust to block the sun. Plants died. Because plants died, plant eaters died. Meat eaters died too, from lack of food.
- Lava from volcanoes killed plants. Plant eaters died. This meant meat eaters didn't have enough food and they died too.
- Something in the air or water made some animals get sick and die.

We are still learning about *Stenonychosaurus*. Finding more bones will help us learn more about this smart dinosaur.

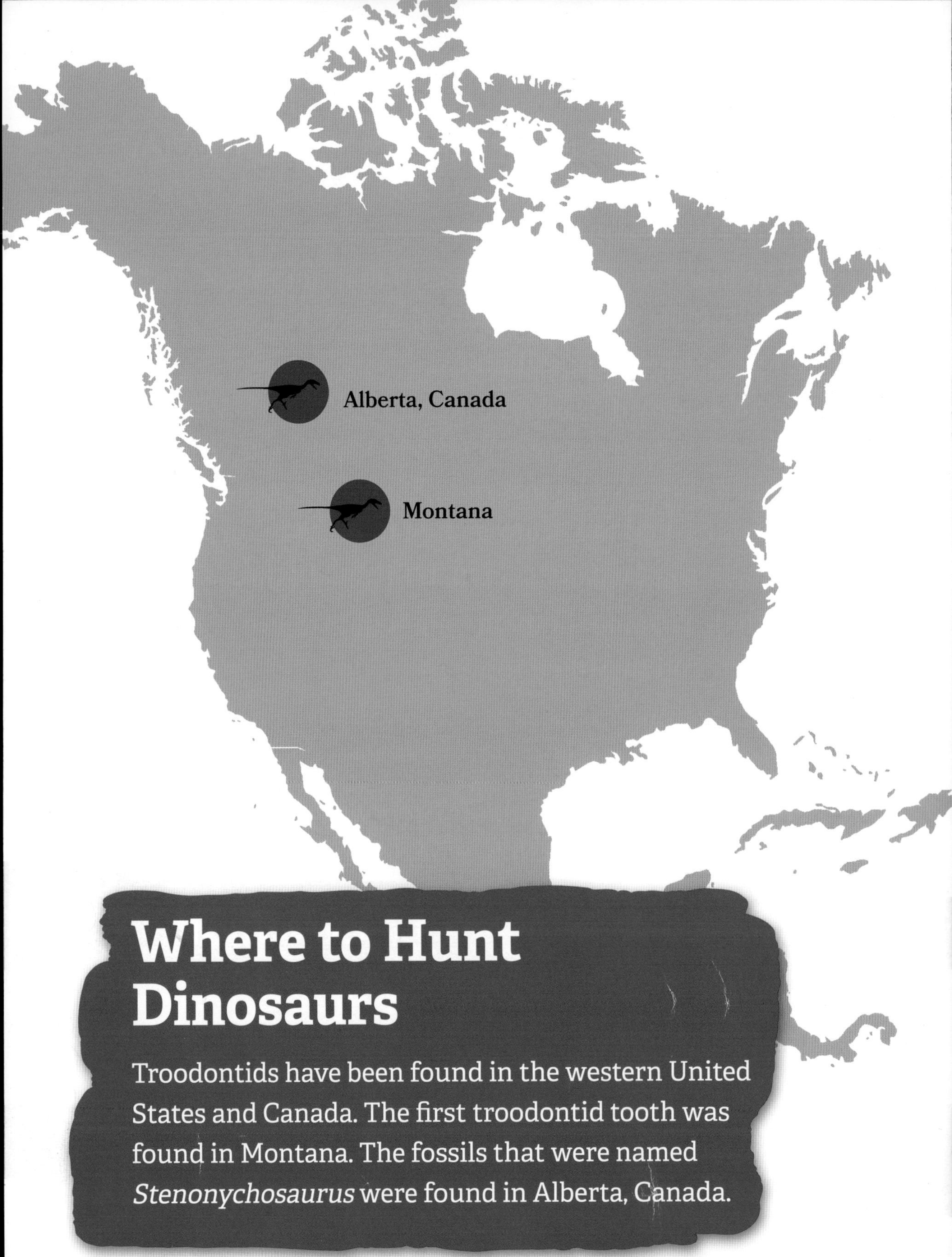

Where to Hunt Dinosaurs

Troodontids have been found in the western United States and Canada. The first troodontid tooth was found in Montana. The fossils that were named *Stenonychosaurus* were found in Alberta, Canada.

Time Line: *Stenonychosaurus* and You

Do you see yourself on the time line? Look at the far right. You live in the Quaternary Period of the Cenozoic Era. Dinosaurs lived in the era before ours. They roamed Earth in the Mesozoic Era.

The Mesozoic Era had three time periods. *Stenonychosaurus* lived in the last one. They were Cretaceous dinosaurs. They lived on Earth about 75 million years ago.

Stenonychosaurus
75 million years ago

YOU!

MESOZOIC			CENOZOIC	
Triassic	**Jurassic**	**Cretaceous**	**Tertiary**	**Quaternary**
251–199.6 million years ago	199.6–145.5 million years ago	145.5–65.5 million years ago	65.5–1.81 million years ago	1.81–NOW million years ago

GLOSSARY

asteroid (AS-tuh-roid): a rock in space

asymmetrical (ay-si-MET-ri-kuhl): not the same on one side as on the other side

balance (BAL-uhns): the ability to keep steady and not fall over

descendants (di-SEN-duhnts): your children, their children, and so on continuing into the future

flesh (flesh): the meat of an animal

fossil (FAH-suhl): a bone or other part of an animal or plant preserved as rock

mammals (MAM-uhls): warm-blooded animals with a backbone

reptile (REP-tile): a cold-blooded, air-breathing animal that has a backbone, lays eggs, and has skin covered with scales or bony plates

sacs (sax): animal or plant parts that are shaped like bags and often hold air or water

wounding (WOOND-ing): hurting the body

INDEX

TEXT-DEPENDENT QUESTIONS

1. What do troodontids have in common?
2. Why was the claw given a different name?
3. How was the size of the skull a clue for scientists?
4. Why do omnivores have both sharp and smooth teeth?
5. Explain how the dinosaur food chain could have changed 65 million years ago.

EXTENSION ACTIVITY

Make salt dough by mixing two parts flour to one part salt in a large bowl. Stir in water until the mixture has a doughy consistency. Knead until smooth and soft. Then, break off small pieces to make *Stenonychosaurus* teeth. Use a toothpick to add ridges. Ask an adult to help you bake the teeth on a cookie sheet in an oven heated to 250 degrees Fahrenheit (121 degrees Celsius) for about two hours until hard. Cool completely before handling your dinosaur teeth.

ABOUT THE AUTHOR

Anastasia Suen is the author of more than 300 books for young readers. Her children were both dinosaur fans, so she took them to the Natural History Museum of Los Angeles County and the La Brea Tar Pits often. They called both of these sites the "dinosaur" museum!

www.rourkeeducationalmedia.com

PHOTO CREDITS: Cover and Title Page ©Joe Tucciarone ; Pg 4 ©Wiki, debibishop; Pg 5 ©Joseph Leidy @ Wiki, Denys; Pg 6 ©American Museum of Natural History Library; Pg 8 ©Wiki ; Pg 9 ©Wiki; Pg 10 ©Ribbet32 @ Wiki; Pg 12 ©Andrey Kuzmin; Pg 13 ©brian @ Wiki; Pg 14 ©Ballista @ Wiki; Pg 15 ©Scott Hartman @ Wiki; Pg 16 ©Todd Marshall ; Pg 18, 25 ©FunkMonk @ Wiki; Pg 18 © John Conway @ Wiki; Pg 19 ©Davide Bonadonna; Pg 20 ©novielysa; Pg 21, 22 ©Jan Sovak; Pg 23 ©Yale Peabody Museum; Pg 26 ©solarseven; Pg 28, 29 ©Scott Hartman @ Wilki; Pg 28 ©ChrisGorgio

Every effort was made to contact copyright holders of materials reproduced within this book. Any omissions will be amended in subsequent reprints if proper notice is provided to the publisher.

Edited by: Kim Thompson
Cover design by: Rhea Magaro-Wallace
Interior design by: Janine Fisher

Library of Congress PCN Data

Stenonychosaurus / Anastasia Suen
(North American Dinosaurs)
ISBN 978-1-73161-451-3 (hard cover)
ISBN 978-1-73161-246-5 (soft cover)
ISBN 978-1-73161-556-5 (e-Book)
ISBN 978-1-73161-661-6 (ePub)
Library of Congress Control Number: 2019932151

Rourke Educational Media
Printed in the United States of America,
North Mankato, Minnesota